AWESOME!

CRAIG SHUTTLEWOOD

CAPSTONE EDITIONS
a capstone imprint

Awesome! is published by
Capstone Editions, a Capstone imprint
1710 Roe Crest Drive
North Mankato, MN 56003
www.mycapstone.com

Library of Congress Cataloging-in-Publication data
is available on the Library of Congress website.

ISBN: 978-1-68446-013-7

Designer: Kay Fraser

Printed and bound in China.
306

This is Marvin. He's a moose.

This is Woody. He's a beaver.

Marvin and Woody are best friends.

One day, Marvin rescued a forest friend from danger.
It was awesome!

The story of Marvin's brave act spread throughout the forest. After that, the brave moose became a local hero.

Being a hero took a lot of work.
Luckily Woody was on hand to help.

Woody made a cape.

Marvin made signs.

AWESOME FOR HIRE

Being awesome takes zen-like focus, stamina, and body conditioning.

Marvin trained every day with his best friend by his side.

It didn't take long before Marvin received his first call for help.

After that Marvin went from local hero to forest celebrity and a statue was built in appreciation of his awesomeness.

ACORN TIMES

Marvin meets fans on day off.

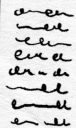

I ♥ MARVIN

MARVIN WINS!
(Moose of the year)

MARVIN
+
WOODY
FRIENDS
FOREVER?

MARVIN CATCHES RACCOON RED HANDED

DIAMOND RETURNED

EXTRA ★

Marvelous Moose saves Squirrel.

FOREST NEWS

Ordinary Moose becomes Awesome

Meanwhile, Woody was missing his old friend
who was now far too popular to spend time with
him. In fact, Woody was feeling quite left out.

"All I ever hear is how great Marvin is! I can
do great things too!" Woody muttered.

But nobody was listening.

Woody decided to get some
attention of his own.

Things quickly spiraled
out of control . . .

The following day, a forest meeting was called. More than one
local resident had something not-so-awesome to say about Woody.

Marvin couldn't believe that his friend could be so mischievous! But he agreed to look into it all the same.

Deep in the forest, Woody was up to no good.
Something that would be sure to get him noticed.

Marvin soon realized that his neighbors were right.

Woody hid the evidence of his not-so-good deed. He would be a hero when he found the "missing" statue.

But just as he was about to rest,
he noticed the wagon was rolling
down the hill at top speed!

"Oh no! What have I done?"
Woody cried.

Not too far away, Marvin's antlers tingled
at the sound of a familiar voice.

"Woody!" Marvin yelled when he saw
his best friend running down the hill.
"Grab my cape!"

Marvin leapt into the chaos to save the family of bunnies!
He had arrived just in time, and he was truly awesome.

But Woody noticed not
all the bunnies were rescued.
He let go of Marvin's cape
and dived into action!

After the excitement, Woody and Marvin sat down to talk.
Woody explained how he wanted some attention
because he was feeling left out. He really was
sorry for all the trouble he had caused.

"Woody, you may have caused
the chaos, but you helped me save
the day," Marvin pointed out.

"I suppose I did," Woody
replied, suddenly starting to
feel awesome too.

The drama was over and there was no real harm done. Except, of course, to the statue.

"I can fix this!" Woody yelled.

And he set to work in a wood-chomping frenzy to reveal . . .